VAASTU

WHAT NO ONE ELSE IS TALKING ABOUT

Change Your Directions Change Your Life

VAASTU
WHAT NO ONE ELSE IS TALKING ABOUT
Change Your Directions Change Your Life

Vikass Sood

Worldwide Published by
Pendown Press

PENDOWN PRESS LLP

An ISO 9001 & ISO 14001 Certified Co.,

Regd. Office: 3767A, Kanhaiya Nagar,

Tri Nagar, Delhi-110035

Ph.: 8130886000, 9650072927, 8595249536

E-mail: info@pendownpress.com

Branch Office: 1A/2A, 20, Hari Sadan, Ansari Road,

Daryaganj, New Delhi-110002

Ph.: 011-45794768

Website: PendownPress.com

Edition: 2025

ISBN: 978-93-6338-579-5

Layout and Cover Designed by Pendown Graphics Team
Printed and Bound in India by Thomson Press India Ltd.

Table Of Contents

Acknowledgements   i

To Whom This Book is Beneficial   ii

About Me   iii

How This Book Can Help   iv

The Role of Faith and Science   v

Why Should You Read This Book?   vi

My Clients   vii

My Promise   xi

CHAPTER 1   THE ESSENCE OF VEDIC VASTU   1

CHAPTER 2   THE FIVE ELEMENTS OF VASTU   4

CHAPTER 3   HOW ASTROLOGY AND
            NUMEROLOGY IMPACT US   8

CHAPTER 4   NORTH-EAST CORNER: THE WATER   11

CHAPTER 5   SOUTH-EAST CORNER: THE FIRE   15

CHAPTER 6   SOUTH-WEST CORNER: THE EARTH   18

CHAPTER 7   NORTH-WEST CORNER: THE AIR   23

CHAPTER 8   CENTRE: THE SKY   26

Big Promise   29

Some Perfect Examples of Vastu   30

Vastu in Your Life   32

Important Points and Frequently Asked Questions   33

⊘ ⊘ ⊘ ⊘

Acknowledgements

My parents, Late Shri Raghbir Singh Sood and Mrs. Satish Sood, are my greatest role models. Their unwavering love, guidance, and values have brought me to where I am today. I am truly grateful for everything they have done.

To my brother, Naveen Sood, you have supported me since childhood and have always been my pillar of strength. Thank you for being there for me and believing in me every step of the way.

To my wife, Vasuda Sood, who has stood by me in every situation. You have handled all family responsibilities with great skill and dedication. Thank you from the bottom of my heart.

To my children, Mansshika Sood & Prranav Sood, who are the source of my happiness and inspiration. Sending you lots of love!

To my team at Vastu_Vikass1 who have been like partners, mentors, and family. Thank you for walking this journey with me.

To our customers, who have shared their experiences and knowledge with us during this journey—thank you for trusting us and being our inspiration.

To my friend, Mr. Dinesh Verma, CEO of Pendown Press, and his team, who supported us throughout this creative process and provided great suggestions.

To the universe for giving me the ideas and strength to complete this book. I am grateful for the love, support, and guidance at every step.

And finally, to all my loved ones who have been with me on this journey—thank you for your unwavering support, encouragement, and affection. Even if your names are not mentioned, you always hold a special place in my heart.

Without the support of all of you, it would not have been possible for me to move forward with confidence.

To Whom This Book is Beneficial

This book is for those who seek growth in their life. It is beneficial for every businessman, regardless of whether they run a small or large business. This book does not discriminate based on caste, creed, or background; it is meant for every human being. If you wish to grow in your life and achieve prosperity with respect, then this book is for you.

Through this book, you can not only learn Vedic Vastu but also make necessary changes in your home or workplace that can help generate more wealth and foster growth in your life.

About Me

My name is Vikass Sood, and I reside in Khanna, District Ludhiana, Punjab. I was born in 1977 to a family where my father served in the Indian Railways, and my mother was a school teacher. I spent my childhood in Bilga, Phillaur, and Khanna. I have one brother and am blessed with the love and support of my parents and elder brother.

I hold a Ph.D. in Vastu and a Postgraduate degree in Numerology. Over the years, I have built a reputation for trust and reliability among the people who know me.

I started my carrier in business in 1997. My day used to start early—I would clean and open the shop at 7:00 AM, and my brother would join me by 10:00 AM. Back then, my daily target was to earn Rs. 500. In 2000, I got married into a wonderful family, marking the beginning of a new phase in my life.

However, tragedy struck when a neighbor kidnapped and murdered my cousin. During this time, a Sikh brother from Ludhiana, who was a Vastu consultant, pointed out that the toilet in our house was in the wrong direction, which, according to him, was the root cause of our misfortune. He also mentioned three to four additional points about our house. At first, we dismissed his observations and took things lightly, but similar incidents—such as the untimely death of a friend whose house also had a toilet in the wrong direction—led me to take Vastu a little bit seriously.

By 2000, I began reading extensively about Vastu and eventually completed my Ph.D. in the subject. Alongside my consulting work, I also run a factory under the name Harr Time Mustard Oil, which produces 100% pure mustard oil without any adulteration. I view this as a service to my community.

How This Book Can Help?

I believe that while I cannot personally reach every individual, I can share my knowledge through this book to bring happiness and prosperity to people's lives.

In 2001, I made changes to my house based on Vastu principles. You will be delighted to know that these adjustments transformed my life completely—my journey shifted into top gear. Today, I own a factory, a bank building, and a paint store. My wife successfully manages her own showroom, and we enjoy a modern lifestyle with all the amenities and comforts one could wish for.

The Role of Faith and Science

V

Our God never wishes ill for anyone. As stated in the holy Shrimad Bhagwat Gita, six things are not within our control:

1. Good or Bad
2. Profit or Loss
3. Life or Death

Despite these limitations, we can use Vastu—a science based on universal principles—to bring harmony, happiness, and growth into our lives. Through this book, I aim to guide you step by step in understanding and applying these principles. With 24 years of experience in this field, I am confident that this book will bring positive changes to your life.

Why Should You Read This Book?

You may already have questions in your mind, such as:

➢ Why should I read a book on Vastu?

➢ Doesn't Vastu create fear or myths?

➢ Won't I need to make costly alterations or additions?

➢ Why do different Vastu consultants have conflicting opinions?

➢ What if I identify a defect in my house but can't take any action?

These are valid concerns, and this book addresses them all. I have written it in a way that simplifies Vastu so that even a common person can understand and apply it. Minor and simple corrections are often enough to bring happiness and prosperity into your life.

Overcoming Misconceptions:

Vastu is often surrounded by fear and myths, but it doesn't have to be. This book provides clear, actionable guidance to help you overcome misconceptions and understand key concepts like the significance of the North-East and South-East directions.

If you are open to learning and agree with even one point presented here, you are in the right place. By reading this book carefully and implementing its suggestions at your own pace, you can achieve positive results—even if they start small, with just 1%. Over time, these improvements will multiply.

Remember, Vastu is a science, and I am merely a medium to share its wisdom with you.

My Clients

Take a look at the trust my esteemed clients have placed in my work through these stories of success and satisfaction:

1. I was initially filled with doubts about Vastu and its effects. However, to my amazement, the results were beyond my imagination. Within just 15 days, my son secured his dream job in the UK. Additionally, my business revenue and customer flow saw a remarkable surge. All thanks to Vikass Ji, who not only changed my perspective on Vastu but also guided me on this transformative journey.

   Sh. Vipul Mittal

2. When I started my business, I was very confused about how to get started and how to deal with clients. I had very few clients, and the ones I did have would negotiate a lot. Though money would come in, it never stayed. During that time, I was facing a major dilemma and constantly wondering what the future held—whether I should switch to another line of work or continue putting in the effort here.

   Then, I met Vikas Ji, who holds a PhD in Vedic Vastu and has completed his post-graduation in Numerology.

   I consulted with him, explained my challenges, and he shared some insights related to Vedic Vastu. After making the suggested changes, the results were beyond my expectations. It completely changed the direction of my life. Today, there is a long line of customers waiting for my services. Now, my concern is how to manage so many people at once.

The number of people coming to me has far exceeded my capacity. I guide people on adopting a healthy lifestyle, teach them ways to live a medicine-free life, and help them become more active. However, the demand is so high that there's no fixed number—it just keeps increasing.

If you are also facing any such issues, I strongly recommend reaching out to Vikas Ji directly, without wasting time elsewhere. In my opinion, he is one of the most trusted Vastu consultants in India today. I don't think anyone else offers the same quality or results that he does, nor do I believe there's anyone better than him in this field right now.

- Kapil Gupta
Health & Wellness Coach

3. We manufacture Surface Protection Films and Decorative Films under the names Top Guard and Top Decors with the support of our respective teams. About one and a half years ago, I met Vikass Ji, who holds a PhD in Vedic Vastu, through a common community. From the very first meeting, I felt something different—a unique positive vibe from him. It felt like he doesn't try to manipulate or confuse people, unlike some Vastu consultants I had met earlier.

   He communicates his insights in a straightforward and constructive manner, without any negativity. If something is wrong with your Vastu, he will tell you directly and honestly about the changes needed, without creating unnecessary doubts in your mind. In every sense, "He is a Solution Provider, not a Problem Finder".

   Vikass Ji is a guide who genuinely advises, 'This is the right way to do it.' The problem with many in today's Vastu industry is that they plant unnecessary fears in your mind just to elevate themselves. This forces you to overthink and worry. But with Vikass Ji, there is no such issue.

I strongly recommend consulting Vikass Ji at least once to experience and feel the difference yourself. You will realize what an exceptional and remarkable personality he truly is.

- Sh. Amit Mittal

CEO and Founder of DVM Protect

⊘ ⊘ ⊘ ⊘

A Note Before We Proceed

Before diving deeper, it is essential to understand the concept of Vedic Vastu. This book will help you grasp how Vastu works and how it can benefit you. By the end of this journey, you will see how simple corrections can lead to significant happiness and prosperity.

Not Just Faith, It's Science –
My Vaastu Story

"When you align with the energies of the universe, success is no longer a struggle—it flows effortlessly toward you."

I don't consider my profession just a profession—it is my passion. My dedication to it runs so deep that whenever I come across a business owner in India who feels stuck—whether it's due to low sales, last-minute order cancellations, delayed payments requiring endless follow-ups, struggling to get client meetings, or dealing with factory breakdowns, labor issues, and countless other challenges—I feel compelled to help.

Through my 20 years of study and interactions with numerous such individuals, I have cracked certain codes that allow me to bring real, concrete results using my knowledge of Vaastu. I can relate to these struggles deeply because I, too, faced them when I ran my own business. However, everything changed when I started studying Vaastu. I delved into ancient Indian scriptures, researching texts that have existed for thousands of years. But I didn't just study them superficially—I immersed myself so deeply that I would often venture into mountains and forests to truly understand their essence in nature's presence. Even in 2024, I embarked on a journey for this exploration, as shown in the picture below. I firmly believe that Vaastu is something that must be practiced with sincerity, hard work, and pure intentions. Unfortunately, in our country, every street has someone claiming to be a Vaastu expert, often misleading people for personal gain.

I also feel that the energy shifts I bring to others inevitably affect me as well—both positively and negatively. That is why I continue to explore these forces, ensuring I understand them on a deeper level. Every six months, I embark on such journeys, engaging in deep meditation and spiritual practice to unlock the hidden mysteries of Vaastu. The moment these principles are applied, profound transformations begin to take place in people's lives.

Perhaps this is why, in such a short time, I have built a name for myself—something that usually takes others decades. While many experts with 20 years of practice charge ₹20 lakh for a consultation, I have been able to achieve similar success within just two years. In fact, people often go so far as to offer me blank cheques, simply requesting a consultation. By God's grace, my schedule remains fully booked 25 days in advance, with clients willingly paying consultation fees upfront and waiting for their turn.

This is not arrogance—it is gratitude. Gratitude toward the people who trust me, toward the divine that has blessed me with this knowledge, and toward Vaastu itself, which has transformed both my life and the lives of my clients.

I share my real story with you so that we can rekindle our faith in India's ancient wisdom—knowledge that was already highly advanced even 2,000 years ago. When you truly connect with it—heart, mind, and soul—you will witness remarkable positive results. The more you believe in it, the more recognition, respect, and success you will receive in return.

My Promise

Through this book, I make the following promises to you:

1. **Understanding Building Orientation**

   You will learn how to calculate the exact degree of your building. This is not an easy task; it took me 15 years of dedicated effort to master this. Yet, it is one of the most important questions in every person's mind when it comes to Vastu.

2. **Financial Growth Through Direction Correction**

   I promise that if you make the necessary corrections to the directions in your building as per Vastu principles, you can attract more wealth and financial success.

3. **Sharing My Expertise**

   I will share the invaluable experience I have gained during my journey of studying and practicing Vastu. You have invested your precious time in reading this book, and it is my duty to ensure you get maximum benefit from it.

So, grab a cup of tea or coffee, sit back, and let's begin this journey together.

CHAPTER 1

The Essence of Vedic Vastu

Vastu Shastra, a profound science rooted in ancient Indian wisdom, has many books available in the market. One of the key texts is the **Vishvakarma Parkash Granth**. Vastu Shastra, born in India, has identical systems in other parts of the world, such as **Divine Wisdom** and **Geomancy** in the West, **Bio-Biology** in America, and **Feng Shui** in China. At its core, Vastu is directly linked to architecture, focusing on the proper alignment of air and light in a building.

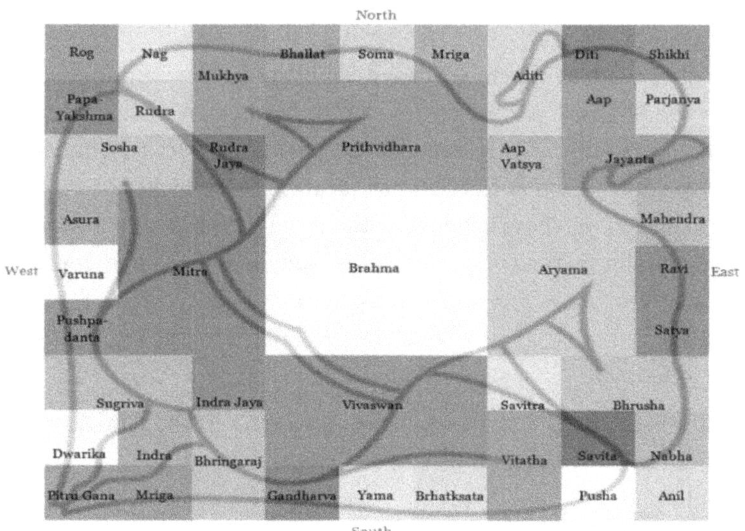

To understand Vastu, let's start with a simple example. Our Shastra defines **4 main directions**, **4 sub-directions**, and other points such as the **Sky** and **Under Earth World**. When you search for a

Vastu Purusha photo online, you'll see a figure with 81 boxes. Each of these boxes represents different aspects of Vastu energy.

Energy and Rays in Directions

In Vastu, when a plot's boundary wall is built, the Vastu Purush is imagined lying on the ground with his head in the North-East, called the "Ishan Kon" and his feet in the South-West, known as the "Nairtya Kon" (नैऋत्य कोण).

Each direction has specific energies or rays. In the North-East, for instance, there are magnetic and electric rays. In ancient times, houses and buildings were designed to let these energies flow freely. If you look at old Havelis, you will see that there was an open space in the middle, surrounded by gates. The people living in these homes were often intellectuals who enjoyed good health, rarely fell ill, and lived longer, happier lives. Our elders often said that the house should face the East, where the sun rises.

Bhagwan Vishvakarma himself highlighted the importance of the Sun in Vastu, and its connection to our lives is undeniable. We should keep the Solar System in mind while constructing a building. You might think that the Sun has no role in our lives, but that's a misconception. There is no life without the Sun. You must be aware that our Earth revolves around the Sun, and the Moon revolves around the Earth. You might think these cosmic cycles don't affect us, but in reality, they have a deeper influence on our lives and surroundings.

Prof. A. E. Duggaless of the Tree Research Institute in America conducted research and discovered that solar radioactivity occurs periodically every 1 year, 11 years, and 90 years. This activity directly impacts the Earth, influencing the formation of tree rings. During these periods, trees strengthen their stems, resulting in the formation of knots—a clear indication of solar radioactivity.

Research On Trees By Ae Dougglas In Tree Research Institute Of America

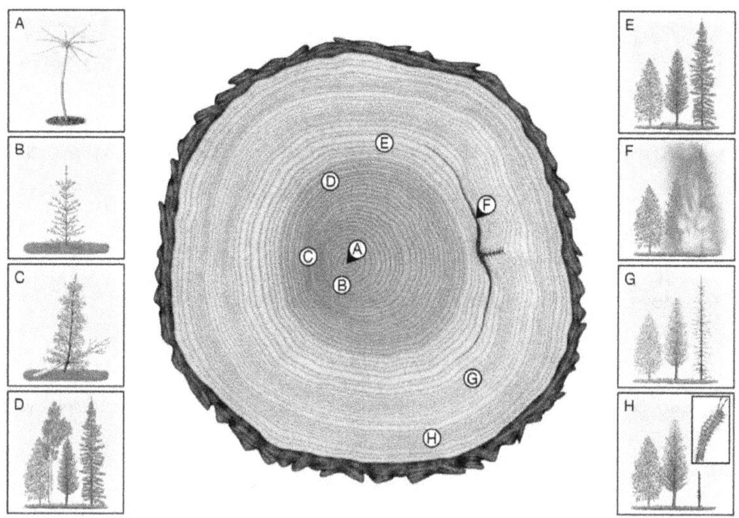

Natural disasters/pandemics, such as COVID-19 and the outbreak of Swine Flu, further highlight the importance of understanding these natural cycles and their profound influence on our lives.

The Five Elements of Vastu

In this chapter, we will explore the five elements, which are fundamental to both Ayurveda and Vastu Shastra. These elements must be in balance to create harmony in our environment. When we build a boundary wall, we divide the space into four sub-directions and one central point, each representing an element.

Here's how the five elements are associated with the directions:

1. **North-East Corner**: This corner, where the North and East meet, represents the **Water** element (Jal).

2. **South-East Corner**: Known as the **Fire Zone**, it is associated with the **Fire** element (Agni).

3. **South-West Corner**: This corner, where the South and West meet, represents the **Earth** element (Prithvi).

4. **North-West Corner**: This is called the **Air Corner**, representing the **Air** element (Vayu).

5. **Center**: The center space represents the **Sky** element (Gagan) and symbolizes balance and harmony.

The five elements can be represented as:

➤ **B** = Bhumi (Earth)

➤ **G** = Gagan (Sky)

➤ **V** = Vayu (Air)

➤ **A** = Agni (Fire)

➤ **N** = Neer (Water)

Balancing these elements properly is called **Vastu**, which helps in creating a harmonious environment for living.

Now, let's understand these one by one:

B = Bhumi (Earth)

The **Earth** element is all about stability and support. It represents the foundation of our life and the physical ground beneath us. A balanced Earth element brings grounding energy, ensuring we feel secure and connected to our surroundings. It is essential for creating a sense of stability and peace in any space.

G = Gagan (Sky)

The **Sky** element symbolizes openness and expansion. It represents the infinite space above us, offering freedom, clarity, and potential for growth. A strong Sky element in Vastu encourages mental clarity, inspiration, and the ability to grow and evolve in life.

V = Vayu (Air)

The **Air** element is associated with movement, communication, and creativity. Air brings fresh energy, new ideas, and vitality. A balanced Air element allows for better flow of thoughts, communication, and opportunities, enhancing the overall dynamism in any environment.

A = Agni (Fire)

The **Fire** element represents energy, transformation, and passion. It is associated with warmth, enthusiasm, and activity. The Fire element brings vitality and a sense of purpose. When balanced, it helps in achieving goals, igniting motivation, and fueling personal and professional growth.

N = Neer (Water)

The **Water** element symbolizes flow, nourishment, and emotion. Just as water sustains life on Earth, it plays a crucial role in balancing energy in our surroundings. Water encourages calmness, relaxation, and emotional stability. A well-balanced Water element enhances prosperity, harmony, and vitality, making it essential for a balanced and peaceful life.

Let's go little bit deeper into this: Perhaps you have heard the name of Nile River, which is the longest river in the world, located in the East. Thousands year back, King Pharaoh of Egypt observed that the river water flowed from higher ground to lower ground. He began recording the river's flow every minute and noticed that when the moon's size changes, it affects the Earth. You may observe high tides when the moon's size increases or decreases.

Vastu affects our lives in similar ways. I believe our life is like a 100-mark exam, and the score is determined by different factors. The first 33% is our **luck**. Suppose three children are born at the same time. One is born in the Ambani family, in a 5-star hospital in Mumbai, another in a small hut behind the same hospital, and the third in a private nursing home. All three will have different life paths because luck plays a role. Luck is based on what we have done in our past lives, and it becomes our present fortune.

The next 33% of our life is determined by our **actions** (Karma). If we don't do good work or actions, our karma score will be reduced. For example, if you treat your employee as a servant and not as a human being, showing disrespect, people will feel cheated, and your karma score will be deducted. This brings us to 66% of our life's score.

You may have seen that some people with **Vastu doshas** still thrive in life. This happens because they have a strong karma score, which helps them flourish despite the Vastu doshas. Now, let's talk about the remaining 33% of our life's score, which is influenced by **Vastu**, **Astrology**, and **Numerology**. Based on my 24 years of experience, I have observed that Vastu plays a bigger role than the other two. But how do Astrology and Numerology affect us?

Curious? We'll talk more about this in the next chapter, so keep reading!

CHAPTER 3

How Astrology and Numerology Impact Us

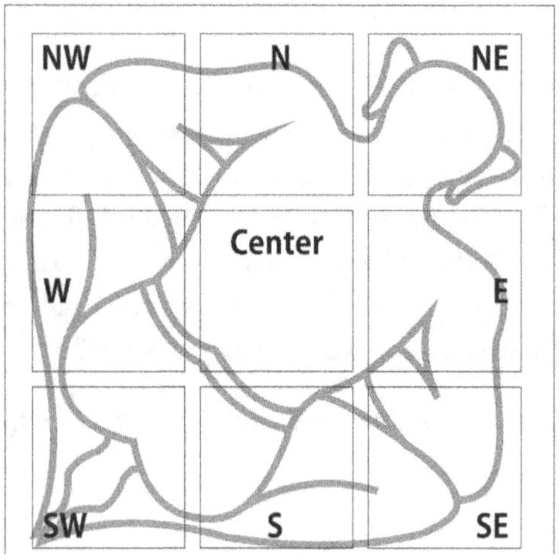

Picking up from where we left you curious, this chapter will finally give you the answers you've been waiting for.

Consider this example: You want to travel from Ludhiana to Delhi by road. You have two options – you can either go in an **Alto car** or a **Ferrari car**. The Ferrari has a 5000 CC engine, while the Alto has an 800 CC engine. The Ferrari costs ₹5 crores, and the Alto costs ₹5 lakh. Who decides the price of the car – you, me, or the company?

Of course, it's the company that decides the price. Now, if you were to choose between the two cars, 80% of people would prefer the

Ferrari, while some may apply logic and choose the Alto. You are thinking right. But if there is a puncture in your tyres on the way, will you still make it to Delhi? I don't know what your financial condition is, as decided by fate, but after repairing your punctured tyre, your travel will be easier. This is how Vastu works. So, even though you have 66%, and your vehicle gets punctured, you get it repaired, attracting good things. Despite traffic signals and toll tax plazas, your journey will be smooth, and you'll reach your destination with speed.

The same principle applies to life: Vastu can help smoothen the journey, even when challenges arise. You can assess your own situation and see how this applies to your life.

Understanding Basic Vastu Degree

You can assess your degree yourself.

Let me explain the basic degree in a simple way. First, we have the magnet compass. You can use a phone application for the compass, but it's better to buy a good-quality compass from the market. Also, make sure not to wear any ornaments on your body while using it.

Now, go to the center of your home, office, or factory, and face the main entrance. The degree shown on the compass will be the degree and direction of your house. This is the main direction. Many people think the right degree is inside the house, but that is incorrect. The degree is determined by the direction outside the house, which can range from 0° to 359°.

It is not necessary for your house to be exactly on 0°, 90°, 180°, or 270°. The degree can vary. Pay attention to it seriously.

How to Attract Prosperity and Growth

The question arises: **How can we attract prosperity, financial growth, and a successful career for our children?**

To achieve this, we need to thoroughly study each direction of the house, as the building's design and orientation hold significant values.

Let's dive into how directions can shape our lives and help us attract wealth and prosperity. First, we'll focus on the **North-East Corner (Ishan Cone),** which is linked to water and the Guru Planet.

North-East Corner: The Water

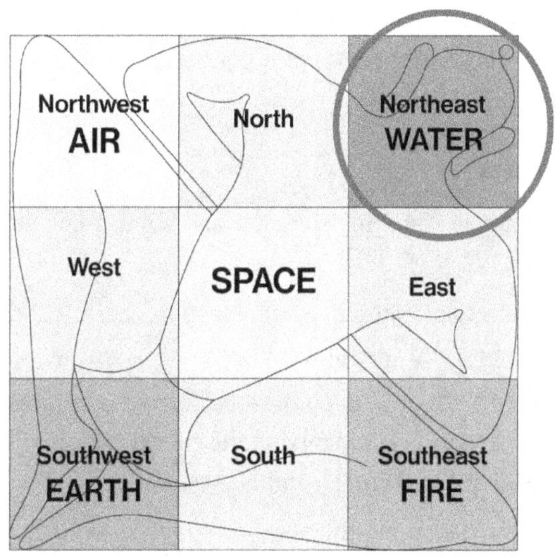

The **North-East Corner (Ishan Cone)** plays a vital role in ensuring prosperity and balance in life. If there is any defect in this corner, then despite your hard work, you may achieve only 10% to 20% of your hardwork. To attract prosperity, follow these essential guidelines:

1. **Underground Water Tank or Borewell**: Ensure there is an underground water tank or borewell in this corner.

2. **Place of Worship**: Establish a place of worship in the East, and ensure you face East while praying.

3. **Light Construction**: Keep the construction in this corner light and minimal.

4. **Cleanliness**: Maintain cleanliness in this area.

5. **Lower Level and Open Space**: The level of this corner should be lower than the South-West and should remain open.

If these conditions are met, you can get many things in life.

Why is the North-East Corner Important?

This direction is one of the most significant in any house. Based on my observations, 80% to 85% of homes with defects in this corner face major challenges.

No Bedroom

➢ This corner is weak for sleeping and should not be used as a bedroom.

➢ Married couples should avoid sleeping here, as this corner relates to God and spiritual energy.

➢ Girls should also not sleep here because they represent Venus (South-East corner), and mixing the energies of fire (Venus) and water (North-East) creates imbalance.

➢ Those who sleep in this corner may experience weakened energy, face loss of employment, suffer business losses, or deal with confusion in their lives.

This room is best suited for the seniors of the house, as it aligns their wisdom with the prosperity of the household. Always respect your elders, as their blessings help bring harmony and abundance.

No Kitchen

➢ A kitchen in the North-East corner disrupts the balance, bringing fire to a water-centric zone.

➢ This can lead to health problems for women in the house.

➢ The energy of **Kuber (wealth)** and **Guru (spirituality)**, which is concentrated here, will be negatively impacted.

➢ Financial shortages, loss of prosperity, and hardships for the family may result.

If a kitchen is mistakenly placed in this corner, arrangements must be made to ensure proper air and water flow. Otherwise, the imbalance between fire and water will create disruptions.

No Toilet

If a toilet is located in the North-East corner, it creates significant Vastu defects. Here's why:

➢ **Blocks Positive Energy**: A toilet in the North-East corner blocks the entry of positive energy, spoiling the good condition of the house and diminishing prosperity very quickly.

➢ **Biggest Vastu Blunder**: This is a critical mistake as per Vastu. Such a defect can lead to significant problems with money, health, and overall harmony in the household.

➢ **Solution for Old Houses**: If an old house has a toilet here, don't panic. Stop using the toilet immediately and consult a Vastu expert to make necessary alterations.

➢ **Avoid in New Constructions**: While building a new house, ensure no toilet is placed in the North-East corner, as it can lead to financial losses, career stagnation, and health issues.

Consequences of Vastu Defects in the North-East

Defects in the North-East corner can lead to several issues:

➢ **Health Problems**: Most of your money will be drained on diseases and unnecessary expenses.

➢ **Career Confusion**: Children may struggle with career choices, and progress may come to a standstill.

> **Business Losses**: Business owners may face loss of customers and profits, and wealth may be wasted on unproductive expenses.

Personal Experience

Here, I am sharing my personal experience that after completing graduation in 1997, I had only one mission—to get rich and achieve something in life. We both brothers were working hard from dawn to dusk and were able to earn only Rs. 500/-. As mentioned earlier, in the year 2000, there was a kidnapping incident involving us. After this, we corrected the toilet in our house, and today, touchwood, I have all the facilities and amenities that a rich person requires.

Therefore, do not have a toilet here. Heavyweight items should also not be stored in this corner. You should be aware that the North-East corner is the head of the Vastu Purusha. If I put heavy weight on your head, would you be able to travel more than 10 meters? You might manage for a short distance but not for a long time. Therefore, it is advised to keep this area light and avoid using it for storage.

In the upcoming chapter, we'll explore the powerful South East direction and its impact on your space and life. Stay tuned for some insightful tips on how to harness its energy!

South-East Direction: The Fire

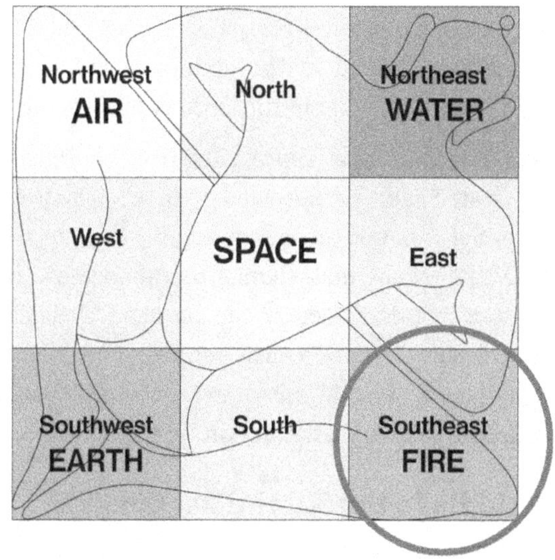

The South-East corner is where the East and South meet. This direction is ruled by the Fire element and Venus planet. It is one of the most important directions in the home and is connected with the luxury of life. Any fault in this direction can directly impact our lives.

I want to share an experience I had during a visit to a house in Patiala (Pb). They told me that they used to own a BMW and a Mercedes, but now they only have a Swift car. Initially, I couldn't identify any fault in their house, and I was tensed about how this could happen. But soon, while I was having tea at their house, the maid mentioned that they had been facing a space shortage 7-8 years ago and had constructed a basement, which they now use as a storage area. I immediately told them, "Please remember that after the construction of the basement, you started losing prosperity." Their response was, "Yes, that is true."

Now it was clear: this direction is closely related to prosperity. No basement should be constructed in this direction. Furthermore, there should not be any toilet in the South-East corner, as it is the area of Venus. Women in our house represent Venus, and therefore, ladies often face problems related to the abdomen and gynaecological issues. Thus, any construction in this area is prohibited.

The South-East corner also represents fire, so never build an underground water tank or borewell here. You may construct a bedroom here, but it is not recommended for boys to sleep in this room because their voice may change to sound more like that of girls. A bedroom in this direction can be used by bachelors, but for married couples, it may cause tension and daily quarrels. Therefore, it is better to avoid this direction if possible. Also, avoid constructing a staircase in this direction, as it can lead to problems.

What Should Be in the South-East Corner?

The South-East corner is the fire zone of the building, making it hotter than other parts of the house. Therefore, the kitchen is the best place to construct in this corner. You might have heard from our elders that they place utensils in the sun after use to allow the sun to burn away any bacteria. This is because the Sun's energy is beneficial, and the South-East direction is ideal for such practices.

This corner is known as the **Agni Cone** (Fire zone) and represents the power of fire. Air also plays an important role here, as it flows from the North-East to the South-East. In case of a fire in the house, it prevents the fire from spreading further in the building.

Therefore, if the kitchen is constructed in this direction, it can help increase prosperity.

In this direction, you can also place a generator set, transformer, inverter, and battery.

And now, let's move on to the next chapter—the South-West corner! This corner is all about stability and balance, like the solid foundation of a good house, office, or factory. So, let's see what makes this direction so special!

CHAPTER 6

South-West Corner: The Earth

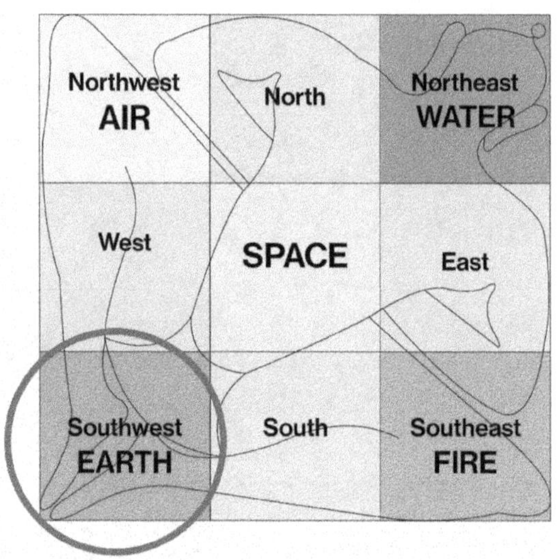

The South-West corner is a very important zone in the house, as it is where the South and West meet. This corner is also referred to as the Naratya Cone (नैऋत्तय कोण) and is equally significant as the Eshan Cone.

Here are some things you should avoid placing in this area:

1. No Toilet in the South-West Corner

It is crucial that no toilet is constructed in this corner. In my 24 years of experience, I have seen that if there is a toilet in this corner, the growth in the lives of the inhabitants stops. This corner is also called the "Corner of Stability." Here lie the feet of Vastu Purush, and it is related to the Earth element. If you build a toilet here, your name, fame, and respect will come to an end. If there is a toilet in this corner, you will face money problems and issues in relationships. Let me clarify with an example: Imagine you are wearing a pair of expensive shoes worth Rs. 1.00 lac and are heading to an important business meeting. Suddenly, your shoes step into human waste, causing a foul smell. As a result, you will not succeed in the meeting, and the opportunity you were hoping for will be lost. In the past, toilets were built in the havelis and houses, but no toilets were constructed inside. Nowadays, people build toilets in adjoining rooms, which is acceptable, but make sure it is not in the South-West (Nairtya Cone).

2. **Borewell, Water Pump, or Water Tank**

This corner relates to the Earth element. Since the earthen factor lies here, water should not be placed in this area. Having a bore well, water pump, or underground water tank in this corner will hinder your growth.

I once visited a house that followed Vastu principles up to 60%. However, there were constant quarrels among family members, their customer flow was significantly low, and the growth of their children was stagnant. After deep discussions and careful study, I discovered that they had a bore well in the South-West Corner, which was the root cause of their problems.

The family was extremely frustrated—one daughter was repeatedly attempting to clear her UGC NET exam but could not succeed, and their elder daughter, of marriageable age, could not find a suitable match. Relations between the father and son were strained, and their younger son's hospital in Ludhiana was running at a loss.

When they shifted the water pump to the correct direction, their lives changed for the better. Therefore, I strongly advise against making such blunders while constructing a new house.

3. Employees' Office/Servant Room

This is a powerful corner. The people who sit here or stay here are seen as owners, and they start making their own rules, which can suppress the actual owner or employer. If an employee stays in this corner, he will slowly start behaving like the owner of the place.

I'll share an example from Ludhiana. A renowned Ayurvedic doctor came to me with a problem. Their only son wanted to leave the family. When I asked about their family history, I found out that the servant had been given the South-West Zone bedroom. The servant started acting smart, trying to create differences in the family, and believed he could become the owner one day. I suggested shifting the servant to another room. Once they did that, the servant left the house, and the family's good times returned.

In the same way, in business premises, the owner should never sit in the area meant for employees. If you do that, your employees won't obey you, they'll create problems, and your business will start going downhill.

4. Open Spaces Should Be Less

Make sure this area has very little open space under the sky; otherwise, you or your family might face problems. This corner should be less open, and the ground level here should be higher than the Eastern side (Eshan Cone).

The reason is simple: in the North-East Corner, the rays of the rising sun are beneficial for us, while the rays of the setting sun can be harmful. That's why the South-West area should not have too much open space.

5. Temple (Place of Worship)

No temple or place of worship should be built in the South-West corner of a house or office. If you look at a plot, the North, East, and center are associated with good energies, while the center to South is connected to negative energies.

Building a temple in this area can disturb the balance and bring unhappiness into life. So, avoid constructing a place of worship here to maintain peace and happiness in your surroundings.

6. Kitchen in Nartaya Cone (नैऋत्य कोण)

Building a kitchen in the South-West (Nartaya Cone) corner brings too many problems. Women in the house, who spend most of their time in the kitchen, may develop a quarrelsome nature and suffer from health issues, particularly in the lower abdomen.

Additionally, this corner represents the Earth element, and placing fire here disrupts stability. This leads to financial troubles, increased loans, and overall instability in the household.

Hence, it is strongly advised not to construct a kitchen in this corner to avoid such issues.

What Should Be in the South-West Corner?

1. Bedroom or Office for the Head of the Family

The head of the family should have their bedroom or office in this corner. This placement creates stability and ensures consistent growth and success in their life.

2. Staircase

A staircase in the South-West corner is ideal, as it helps cover the maximum land area and adds weight to this corner. Houses with staircases here often experience growth and stability. If you want to test this, try selling your product to a customer whose house has a staircase in the South-West. You will likely notice faster sales and higher profits.

3. Storage Room

This corner is suitable for building a store or storage room. Placing heavy materials here will lead to success and stability in your life and business.

4. Water Tank

Different Vastu consultants have varying views on water tanks in this corner. In my opinion, a water tank should ideally not be placed here. However, storing water for daily use in small amounts can be acceptable.

Our next chapter is about the North-West Corner: The place where the winds of change blow—sometimes gently, sometimes like a hurricane!

Let's explore this fascinating corner in the next chapter.

North-West Corner: The Air

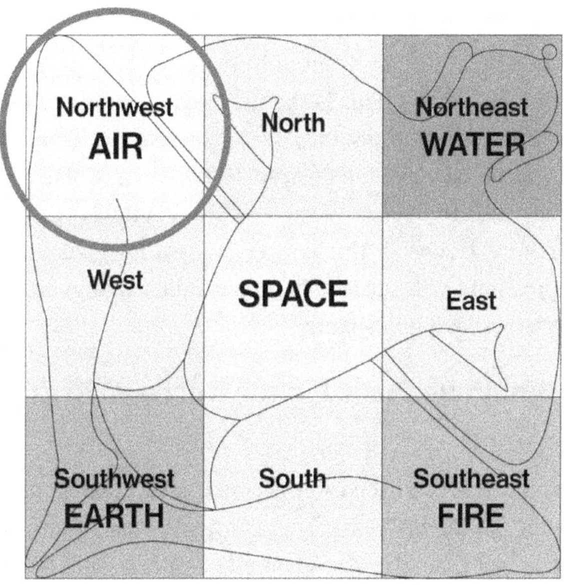

The North-West corner, also known as the **Air Corner**, which signifies a direct connection with the **Air Element**. This corner holds significant importance in terms of relationships. Any fault or imbalance in this corner can negatively affect your personal relationships.

What Should Not Be Placed in the North-West Corner?

1. Bore Well

Avoid constructing a **bore well** in the North-West corner. This placement can create disturbances in your relationships and lead to potential **court cases**. It can negatively affect your family and personal life. Therefore, it is crucial to ensure no underground water storage in this corner.

2. Main Person Bed room

The head of the family should not have their bedroom in the North-West corner. This is the Air Corner, and if the head of the family stays here, they may feel disconnected from the house and will not achieve the desired 100% success. The North-West corner rules the South-West, so it's not suitable for the head of the family. However, this corner is ideal for girls' rooms. Girls sleeping here will succeed in their studies, find good marriages, and attract loving husbands.

What Should Be Placed in the North-West Corner?

1. Kitchen

While the South-East corner is considered the best place for the kitchen, the North-West corner can also be used for this purpose. This is because the Air element supports the Fire element, and since Air is essential for Fire, this corner can serve as an alternative location for your kitchen.

2. Bathroom & Toilets

You may build a **bathroom** or **toilet** in the North-West corner. This direction is good for toilets. However, when using the toilet, ensure that your face is directed towards the **North** or **South**.

3. Stairs

The North-West corner is a good option for constructing **stairs**. It aligns with the energy flow of the house and is considered beneficial.

It's time to talk about the last corner — the center corner! Let's not keep you waiting any longer and see how this space affects our daily lives.

Centre: The Sky

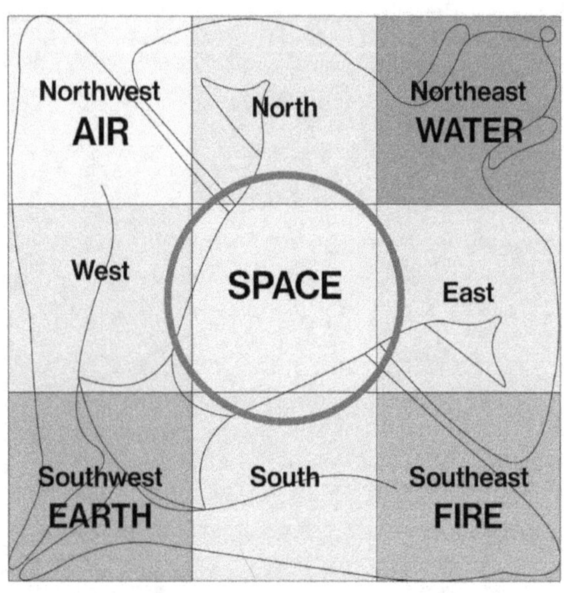

The center of your home, often called **Brahm Sthan**, holds great significance in Vastu Shastra. It is considered the heart of the house, representing balance, harmony, and stability. Just like water, which brings life and nourishment, the center of the house has the power to influence the energy and well-being of everyone who lives there. Let's explore the importance of this central space and the guidelines that can help bring positive energy to your home.

Space or Brahm Sthan

The center of the house, known as Brahm Sthan, is a very sensitive area, both in homes and offices. It is highly recommended not to construct a basement here. I would like to share a personal experience: I once visited a client's house where the center of the house was lowered, and they were using it as a drawing room. The family was facing numerous problems in their life. One of the sons believed in Vastu, while the other did not. I visited their house and observed several issues. While sitting in the drawing room with the younger son, I suggested filling the lowered area with soil temporarily. I told them that if they were open to trying something new, they could see the positive change in their life. They agreed, and their life turned around dramatically. Today, they own three factories, and the younger son has become one of my best clients.

If there is a basement in the center of your house, fill it temporarily with soil. This will correct any Vastu dosh and bring positive results. This approach is rooted in science. Any plot with boundary walls is considered a Vastu Purush, and if weight is placed in the center, it disturbs the balance and energy flow, which negatively affects the household. Therefore, it is highly advised to fill the center or consult a Vastu expert to address the issue effectively.

Stairs/Heavy Construction in Brahm Sthan

Just as a disturbed abdomen affects the ability to live a normal life, placing heavy weight in the Brahm Sthan (the center of the house) can cause issues related to the abdomen and back. If stairs or heavy construction is placed in this area, it will lead to health problems. Therefore, avoid placing heavy structures in the center of the house.

When constructing your home, it is best to keep the center open to the sky. This will allow sunlight to enter the entire house and help reduce electricity consumption. You can see examples of such constructions in Haridwar dharamshalas, where the center is left open to the sky. Despite having fewer amenities, the natural light and energy flow make it a comfortable place for people. This example shows the benefits of leaving the center open to the sky, and the positive impact it has on the comfort and harmony of the space.

Big Promise

I have promised to you that I will share my experience in this book, which is the result of my continuous hard work and practice, on how we can make our directions correct. I am thankful to the readers of this book and, on the other hand, I am grateful to my parents, mentors, teachers, and my loving wife, Vasuda Sood, and my children, who made it possible for this book to be printed. Now the time has come to teach you about directions. Would you like to learn?

When you want to buy land, you should stand in the center and face the road. Then hold a compass in your hand. You can use the compass application on your phone for the time being, but a professional compass will give the best results. Note the degree. Some people use the compass outside the plot, but that will lead to incorrect results. For accuracy, you should stand in the center of the plot.

One more thing you should keep in mind: there should be no iron material or power cables passing through the plot. This will affect the accuracy of the degree according to Vastu principles.

Some Perfect Examples of Vastu

Triputi Balaji

Triputi Balaji Temple is a good example. In this temple, the North East has a water pond and, in the Southwest, there are high mountains. The mandir is constructed as per Vastu principles. Here, people have a partnership with God and they succeed in their missions. In this temple, money and offerings are much higher than in other temples.

North & South Korea

North Korea and South Korea were partitioned in 1948, one-part North Korea and the other South Korea. In North Korea, there is the Yalu River in the south direction, which is a fault according to Vastu. Just opposite, South Korea's north has this river, which contributes to its growth. According to Vastu, a water source in the North is good, and therefore, it signifies growth for the country.

How Beneficial the Book Is for You After Reading It

I believe that Vastu is a science and a universal truth. The idea that it is useful for some and not useful for others is a myth. Vastu has a direct relation to the Sun, Air, and Water. The Sun treats everyone equally. I feel lucky if a single person's life is changed after reading my book. If you do any work yourself and have little knowledge of Vastu, you will definitely get results.

For example: 9 + 0 = 9.

If you have a friend who has knowledge of Vastu, it will definitely affect your results.

For example: 9 + 9 = 18.

If you have an expert, the result will be:

For example: 9 x 9 = 81.

Keep the degree in mind.

Some people say that there is no result. Then, I want to tell you that the degree should be 100% correct. If the degree is mismatched, then our results will change. For example, if an airplane is flying from Delhi to Hyderabad and it is off by 20 degrees, it will reach Pune instead of Delhi. Therefore, we have to calculate the degree accurately. In my opinion, help should be taken from a Vastu expert for better and more accurate results.

Vastu in Your Life

First off, I hope you've enjoyed this journey through the world of Vastu. If you're now thinking, "Wow, I never knew my house/office could have so much power!"

I hope you've learned some valuable tips that you can actually use to improve your space and life.

Still, you have any questions, need more information, or would like to share any feedback, feel free to **schedule a meeting with me**.

Email: vastuvikass1@gmail.com

Whether you want to understand something from the book more deeply or need help with Vastu, I'm here to help, answer your questions, and maybe even share a few more Vastu secrets along the way.

With Regards,

Vikass Sood

Important Points and Frequently Asked Questions

1. **Where should the boker be placed?**

    It should be placed in the South West area. Never place the boker in the North East corner.

2. **Where should the cash chest be placed?**

    North is the place of Kuber, the God of wealth, but some Vastu consultants may suggest the North East. However, with my 24 years of experience, I have found that the South West corner brings more stability to wealth. If you keep cash in the South West, it will create more stability and increase over time.

3. **Where should the worship place be, and which direction should one face while worshiping?**

    The place of worship should be in the North East corner. To bring prosperity and peace in life, you should face the East while praying.

4. **What size of statues or pictures of God should be placed in the place of worship?**

    You should place a photo or statue of Goddess Lakshmi in a sitting position, where her hand is shown giving money. You can also place a statue or photo of the Shiv Parivar or a photo of your Guru. The size of the photos/statues should not be more than 9 inches. Anything larger than 9 inches should be properly installed as per Hindu rituals in the place of worship.

5. How to control ill health and expenses on medicines?

Clean the floor with salty water every Wednesday and Saturday, and take a bath with salty water on these days. This will provide relief. Advise your family members to follow the same routine.

6. Where should medicines be stored?

Do not place medicines in the South East and South West areas, as this can lead to increased illness. Store them in the North West corner, and disease will be cured more quickly.

7. Where should important papers, such as property registry, be kept?

Important papers like registry documents of your house, factory, and office should be kept in the South West or North East direction. This will ensure growth and stability.

8. Where should garbage and scrap be placed?

Do not place a dustbin at the entrance of the house or in the North East. Always keep garbage in the South West, but avoid digging any pit there.

9. Is a T-shaped plot good?

The answer is no. Based on my experience; I have found that "T" shaped plots are not ideal.

10. How should the husband-and-wife sleep?

The wife should sleep on the left side of the husband because the heart is on the left side. This way, the wife will rule the husband's heart.

11. In which direction should we place our heads while sleeping?

The head should be placed in the South West direction. Since the head is the north pole of the body, placing it in the North direction will create a magnetic push, which can disrupt sleep.

12. What pictures should be placed?

Place pictures that bring happiness. Never place pictures that depict negative thinking or battlefields.

13. Should artificial flowers be kept in the house?

Never place artificial flowers, as they can make relationships artificial.

14. Should we place photos of Gods in the bedroom?

Do not place photos of Gods in the bedroom. The correct direction for them is the North East.

15. Should we buy a south-facing plot?

Yes. God is our ultimate father, and there is no fault in any direction. Just as parents will never think badly of their children, God considers all directions good. The key is to design the house according to Vastu.

16. Which direction is best for the marriage of daughters?

Marriageable daughters should sleep in the North West corner of the house for a quicker marriage.

17. Where should children's study tables be placed?

Always place the children's study table in the West or South West, and they should face East while studying. This will double their results. You can also use the North East direction.

18. Should mirrors be placed in front of the bed?

Avoid placing a mirror in front of the bed where your body is reflected, as this can disrupt sleep. It may also cause health issues, especially for women.

19. How to control maids and labor?

To reduce labor turnover, avoid letting them sit in the North West. You can also give them some sweets on Saturdays.

20. Where should photographs/pictures of our ancestors be placed?

The North East corner is related to God, so place photos or pictures of your ancestors in the South West corner, just opposite to it. Never place them in the place of worship.

21. Should we place a Nazarbattu or photo of God outside the house?

Never do this. You won't see any Nazarbattu on luxury cars or expensive buildings; it's just a myth.

22. Should construction residue be placed on top of the house?

Do not place construction residue on the roof, as it can harm your planets. How can you live if your head is burdened with heavy weight?

23. Which direction should we face while eating meals?

Your face should be in the East direction. If possible, eat your meals while sitting on the ground.

24. Which direction should the bedroom of husband and wife avoid?

Newlywed couples should avoid sleeping in the North East corner, as it can lead to tension in their relationship and issues with conceiving children.

25. Do our names have an impact on numerology?

Yes, they do have an impact.

26. Which direction should "Tulsi" be planted?

"Tulsi" can be planted in the North East, North, or East corners. It can also be planted in the courtyard.

27. Which plants can be planted in the house?

Any plant can be planted in the house, but avoid plants that release white-colored fluid, as it can harm the eyes. Also, avoid planting thorny plants.

28. What should be done for prosperity in the house?

If your parents are alive, touch their feet before leaving the house. If they are no longer with you, offer your respects to their photos. This will bring success.

29. Where should children's books be stored?

The cupboard for children's books should be in the South West. You can also place it in the North East.

30. How to solve the labor problem?

To solve the labor problem, give them sweets on Saturday and salty snacks. This will help reduce labor issues.

31. In which direction should a clock be placed?

The clock should be placed on the North, East, or North East wall of the house.

32. Do affirmations work?

Yes, affirmations are 100% true and will give the desired results.

33. In which wall should mirrors be placed?

Mirrors should be placed on the North East, North, or East wall of the house.